Seasons of the Great Tree

by Michael Scotto
illustrated by The Ink Circle

STARRING

NUEVA O. BOBO
THE REPORTER

One afternoon, at the end of summer, Nueva was walking past the Great Tree.

"I wonder..." she thought. "What makes the Great Tree so great?"

Nueva was a reporter for the Midlandian Times, and every time something caught her attention, she would write about it for the newspaper.

Nueva went to Chief Tatupu, the leader of Midlandia, for answers. "Well, Nueva, the Great Tree is very special," Chief said.

"Long ago, the Great Tree was actually many separate trees. As the years went by, the branches grew together, twisting and turning."

"As the tree limbs wrapped around each other, a single tree began to form, stronger than before. The branches kept working and growing together until they became the Great Tree you see today. They are still working and growing, even now!

"I've never seen it working or growing," Nueva said. "It's always been the same big tree."

"Then perhaps you are not paying enough attention," Chief replied.

Nueva decided that she would do what she always did when something made her curious: she would watch it. She sat down in the shade near the Great Tree with a backpack full of snacks, and she watched. "I'm not going to leave here until you do something," she told the tree.

Days passed.
Nueva watched, ate, and wrote
in her notebook. "But I can't see you
working or growing!" she groaned.
Not only that, but she was out of food.
"I'll be back tomorrow, and something
had better be different."

The next day, Nueva came back and
something was different. **"Your leaves!"** she said.
"They're turning yellow! Are you sick?"

"**Chief! Chief!**" Nueva cried, out of breath. She had run all the way from the Great Tree.

"What seems to be the matter?" he asked.

"**Come look!**" she replied.

"It is part of nature,"
Chief told her, pointing to the
tree. "The leaves change every
year about this time." And off
he went.

But Nueva wasn't sure
she believed him. "I'd better
keep watching," she thought.

Nueva visited the Great Tree every day.
Soon, the leaves weren't just turning yellow.

"They're turning red, brown, and orange, too!" Nueva said.

Red

Orange

Nueva copied every
single one in her notebook.

Brown

Purple

The summer ended and became fall. Now Nueva had to wear a light jacket when she came to watch the Great Tree. **"How are you feeling today?"** she asked the tree. And the Great Tree did something very strange—it dropped one of its leaves to the ground.

Nueva picked up the leaf. It was not soft, like a normal leaf, but crunchy. **"The tree really is sick,"** Nueva thought. "I'd better bring in the professionals." The tree shed several more leaves, which fluttered to Nueva's feet.

"Hurry, Doc," Nueva said. "The Great Tree needs your help."
Doc Fixit lugged her medical bag after her. "I don't think you understand, Nueva. I take care of Midlandians, not trees."
"Please, just look?" Nueva begged.

As Doc looked at the tree, more crunchy leaves fell. "See, Doc?" Nueva said.

Doc just chuckled. "Oh, Nueva... the Great Tree isn't sick. Its leaves drop off every fall."

"**Don't worry,**" Nueva told the tree. "I'll keep an eye on you just the same."

As the fall continued, the leaves piled up and other Midlandians came to play in them. But Nueva just watched until each branch was bare.

Soon, snow began to fall in Midlandia.
Those who didn't have to work came and
played at the Great Tree. They threw
snowballs, made snow-Midlandians, and
played tag around the tree's trunk.

"You don't look very great right now,"
Nueva told the tree. "You don't look very great at all.
You look strange without your leaves," she said.
"And how are you keeping warm?"

The next day, Chief found Nueva wrapping blankets around the trunk of the Great Tree. **"What are you doing?"** he asked, astonished. "Do you have any spare sheets or towels?" she replied. **"I'm all out."**

"Nueva," Chief said, sitting her down. "The Great Tree does not need blankets. In the spring, its leaves will grow back, good as new!" Nueva was doubtful. **"Do you promise?"** she asked. **"I promise,"** Chief told her. "It happens every year. Just watch."

So Nueva watched. The new year came, and soon the snow began to melt off of the Great Tree.

One day, Nueva came to show the tree her new dress. "I'm wearing a new one because I'm too tall for the one I had last spring," she said. Then she saw something that caught her eye. **"Green!"** she cried out. It was a single leaf, sprouting from a branch high up on the Great Tree. Every day, leaves grew back in bunches.

And by the end of the month...

"**All of your leaves are back!**" Nueva said with excitement. "I have to go find Chief."

"**You were right,**" Nueva told Chief. "The Great Tree is great again."

"Actually, Nueva," Chief replied, "the Great Tree was always great, even when its leaves were gone."

"**All things change, all the time. It is a part of life.**"

"You're right, Chief," Nueva said. "The Great Tree is great because it changes every day. So the thing that makes it great is the same thing that makes all of us great, too."

DISCUSSION QUESTIONS

Change is when something is different today than it used to be.

Can you think of something in your life that has changed?

How are things different?

How do you feel about those changes?